PANDA BEAR'S SECRET

by MICHAELA MUNTEAN
illustrated by CHRISTOPHER SANTORO

A GOLDEN BOOK, New York
Western Publishing Company, Inc., Racine, Wisconsin 53404

Panda Bear likes secrets.
He likes to have a secret place
for his favorite toys…

... and a secret drawer
for special treasures.

But most of all, he likes it when someone tells him a secret. He likes to feel that special secret whisper-tickle in his ear.

Panda Bear is a good secret keeper. So when his grandma told him a secret one morning, he didn't tell anyone else.

Later that morning Panda Bear and Grandma went shopping. They came home with one big bag and two little bags.

Panda Bear's mother asked what was
in them. All he said was, "It's a secret."

After lunch Panda Bear and Grandma
went into the kitchen. They wouldn't let
anyone else come in.

When they were finished Mother said,
"What were you two doing in there?" Panda
Bear and Grandma just smiled and said,
"It's a secret."

Panda Bear went to his room and closed the door. Mother could hear a *snip, snip, snip* sound.

When he came out Mother asked him
what he had been doing. All Panda Bear said
was, "It's a secret."

After supper Panda Bear and
Grandma said, "We'll do the dishes."

"Thank you," said Mother.
"That is very nice of you."

Panda Bear and Grandma washed
and dried the dishes quickly.

After they put the dishes away, they took a big cake out of the cupboard. They blew up balloons and hung streamers from the ceiling.

Panda Bear ran to his room. He
pulled a box out from under his bed.

He took a big heart-shaped
card out of his secret drawer.

When Panda Bear came back, Grandma was putting candles on the cake. "It's time to let Mother know the secret," she said.

"Mother," Panda Bear called,
"please come into the kitchen."

"Happy birthday!" cried Panda Bear and Grandma when Mother walked into the room.

"This was the secret," Panda Bear said. "Are you surprised?"

TO MOM

HAPPY BIRTHDAY

"Oh, yes," said Mother, and she gave him a big hug. "You are the best secret keeper I know."